For Thomas J. Bowen III,
The Dean of the Bowen Brothers

Published by
PEACHTREE PUBLISHING COMPANY INC.
1700 Chattahoochee Avenue
Atlanta, Georgia 30318-2112
PeachtreeBooks.com

Text © 2025 by Fred Bowen
Jacket and title page illustrations © 2025 by Marcelo Baez

All rights reserved. No part of this book may be reproduced, transmitted, or stored in an information retrieval system in any form or by any means, graphic, electronic, or mechanical, including photocopying, taping, and recording, without prior written permission from the publisher. Additionally, no part of this book may be used or reproduced in any manner for the purpose of training artificial intelligence technologies or systems, nor for text and data mining.

Design and composition by Lucy Ricketts
Edited by Zoie Konneker

Printed and bound in September 2025 at Sheridan, Chelsea, MI, USA.
10 9 8 7 6 5 4 3 2 1 (hardcover)
10 9 8 7 6 5 4 3 2 1 (trade paperback)
First Edition
HC ISBN: 978-1-68263-412-7
PB ISBN: 978-1-68263-843-9

Library of Congress Cataloging-in-Publication Data

Names: Bowen, Fred, author.
Title: Special teams / Fred Bowen.
Description: First edition. | Atlanta : Peachtree, 2025. | Series: Sports stories | Audience term: Preteens | Audience: Ages 8–12 years. | Audience: Grades 4–6. | Summary: "In football, most touchdowns are scored in two ways. First, give the ball to a player and let him run. Second, the quarterback throws the ball to a receiver who takes it in for the score. Leo wants to be a wide receiver—the player that catches passes and scores touchdowns. But his coach isn't so sure that the position is right for Leo. He must figure out how to help his team in other ways by learning other ways to score. In Special Teams, Leo's team is counting on him to know his strengths and make the right play"— Provided by publisher.
Identifiers: LCCN 2025003292 | ISBN 9781682634127 (hardback)
Subjects: CYAC: Football—Fiction. | Self-actualization | Teamwork (Sports) | LCGFT: Sports fiction. | Novels.
Classification: LCC PZ7.B6724 Sop 2025 | DDC [Fic]—dc23
LC record available at https://lccn.loc.gov/2025003292

EU Authorized Representative: HackettFlynn Ltd, 36 Cloch Choirneal, Balrothery, Co. Dublin, K32 C942, Ireland. EU@walkerpublishinggroup.com

SPECIAL TEAMS

Fred Bowen
SPORTS STORY

Ω
PEACHTREE
ATLANTA

Chapter ONE

Leo Campbell sprinted downfield, dug his right foot into the dry dirt of Sligo Park, and cut into the middle of the field. The football was in the air before Sebastian "Sebby" Bates could call out "Three Mississippi!"

Leo reached out. The ball grazed his fingertips and dangled in the air for a moment. But Leo was off-balance, and he tumbled to the turf with the ball bouncing alongside of him. Leo slammed his palm down, and a small cloud of dust appeared around his hand.

"Good try," Ginny Bruno said as she held out her hand to help Leo up. "That was almost a great catch."

"Yeah, almost," Leo said.

"You had me by a couple steps," Ginny admitted. She reached down and picked up Leo's flag from the ground. Leo tucked the rag into the waistband of his shorts.

"Thanks."

Back in the huddle, Hank Harris apologized for the pass. "Sorry, I led you too much."

"That's okay," Leo said. "But I've got to catch those if I want to play wide receiver for the Newport Raiders' junior varsity team."

Hank laughed. "You're good. I definitely won't be playing quarterback for that team." He looked at Leo. "You want to try quarterback?"

Leo did not have any better luck. After two incomplete passes, he called out, "We're going to punt."

The punt in this four-on-four flag football game meant Leo threw the football downfield as high and as far as he could as his three teammates raced to cover the punt. Ginny gathered in the ball and ran ten yards before Hank pulled the flag from her waist.

"I got you!" Hank shouted as he held the strip of cloth high.

Sebby tossed a couple of quick passes to Ginny to move their team closer to the end zone. "Come on," Leo barked at Abby Bannister. "You have to cover her."

Abby spread her hands out in frustration. "You want to cover Ginny?" she asked. "She's really tough."

"Okay, let's switch." Leo signaled with his hands. He lined up across from Ginny on the next play. A small smile spread along her lips.

"You guys must be getting serious," she said.

"Hut one . . . hut two . . ."

Ginny broke from the line of scrimmage, sprinting straight at Leo. She took one step to the sideline and then cut upfield. Leo fell for the fake for the briefest moment but then spun and chased Ginny along the sideline.

Leo looked back for the football. It was almost there. At the last instant, Leo reached up and tapped the falling football away from Ginny's hands just as she was about to grab it.

"Nice play," Ginny said as the two friends jogged back. "I thought that one was a sure TD."

The game continued. When he was on defense, Leo kept Ginny from catching many more passes. On offense, Leo caught a few passes but also dropped a couple catchable balls.

"Let's take a break," Hank said. "I'm sweating like crazy."

The eight players spread out in the shade beneath a pair of large oak trees near the park. Leo eyed the field, baking in the summer heat.

"Man, it's hot," he said. Then he drained his water bottle.

"It's going to be really hot when you guys are at football tryouts next week in all that equipment," Ginny said, pulling at her shorts. "That's another reason you should stick with flag football. You can play in something cool."

Leo smiled. Ginny kept trying to get him and Hank and Sebby to play on the school's flag football team.

"When are the JV tryouts?" Abby asked.

"Next Tuesday," Sebby said. "But they aren't really tryouts. Coach Carter keeps almost everybody for the junior varsity team."

Leo tilted his water bottle so he could get the last drops. "Yeah, but Coach will split the team into offense, defense, and special teams. You know, the guys who play on punts and kickoffs." He looked at Hank and Sebby. "What position are you guys going to try out for?"

"Definitely not quarterback," Hank laughed. "Anyway, it doesn't matter what I want to play. The moment the coaches see a big guy like me they are going to put me in the line. What about you guys?"

"Defense," Sebby said, almost before the question was out of Hank's mouth. "I would rather do the hitting than be on offense and be the one getting hit."

Ginny noticed Leo hadn't answered the question. "So, what's the deal, Leo? What position are you going to try out for?"

"Wide receiver."

"Then you better not drop any passes," Sebby said.

Hank nodded his head. "Anything you can touch you should catch."

"Maybe you should try out for defensive back," Ginny said. "You did a good job on me out there."

"Maybe," Leo said, although he didn't mean it. He wanted to be a wide receiver, the guy who caught passes and scored touchdowns.

Leo grabbed the football and popped to his feet. "Come on, let's keep playing. Whose ball is it?"

"Ours," Hank said. "They scored last."

Leo and his team gathered in a huddle. Hank took charge, drawing the play on a teammate's chest.

"I'll be quarterback. Abby, you do a down and in from the left. Liam, you hike and flare to the right. Leo, you do a buttonhook and go. On two."

Leo lined up on the right. Sebby was covering him.

"Hut one . . . Hut two . . ."

Leo sprinted ten yards, then slowed down as if he were about to turn toward the quarterback. As Sebby pressed closer, Leo spun past him.

This time the pass was right on target. Leo gathered the ball in full stride, tucking it under his right arm. He ran past the goal line and raised his hands and the football in triumph.

Touchdown!

Chapter Two

Leo stood between Hank and Sebby at the Raiders' first practice as they ran in place, lifting their knees close to their chests. Coach Carter blew his whistle to stop the exercise.

"Ginny was right," Leo said, catching his breath. "I am sweating like crazy under these pads."

"Why do you think the coaches are always after us to drink a lot of water?" Hank asked.

"Hey, we're playing real football now," Sebby said. "Stop whining."

Coach Carter blew his whistle and the players were at it again, doing lunges, squats, and quickness drills.

"Real football?" Leo said after Coach

signaled the players to stop. "Seems like all we are doing is a million exercises."

Hank took a long gulp of water. "Don't worry, Coach is just seeing who is in shape."

Sebby nodded in agreement. "Things will get real . . . real soon."

Coach Carter announced, "All right, I want everybody to split up into position groups. Anyone who wants to play offensive line, go with Coach Dunn."

"That's me," Hank said as he moved away. "See you after practice."

Coach continued the roll call. "Defensive linemen and linebackers go with Coach Rodriguez." Sebby strapped his helmet tight and moved off, saying "good luck" to Leo.

"Wide receivers and defensive backs are with Coach K. . . . Coach Karavetsos. Quarterbacks stay with me. Remember you may not end up playing the position you want to play. All right, let's get to work."

Leo jogged over to where Coach K. was standing. He looked like he was in his twenties with the long arms and legs of a real wide receiver. He was pointing with a football as he said, "I want anyone who wants to play wide receiver over here. Anyone who wants to play defensive back over there."

Most of the players went over to the wide receiver group, while only a few joined the defensive backs.

This might be tough, Leo thought as he noticed a group of taller sophomores standing among the wide receivers.

Coach K. started passing out a sheet of paper to each of the players. Leo glanced down at the sheet.

"This may be review for some of you guys

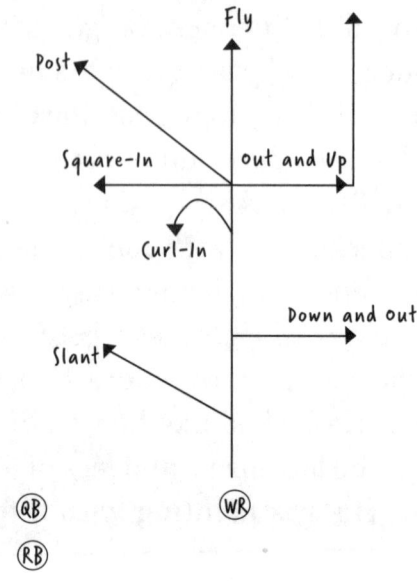

from last year, but these are the basic pass patterns we are going to run this season."

Coach K. took a position near the right sideline. "Let's start with a quick slant from the right," he said, demonstrating the pattern. "Left foot first, take four steps, push off with the right foot. Head and hands up looking for the ball."

He motioned to one of the sophomore receivers. "Jamar, show them how it's done." Jamar Johnson stepped forward and ran the pattern as Coach shouted instructions.

"Remember, come out hard. You want the defense to think you are going long. Push off your right foot even harder. You want to get separation from the defensive back. Head up, hands up."

He waved the group over. "All right, line up."

Each of the wide receivers ran the pattern as a defensive back shadowed the play. On his second time through, the ball bounced off Leo's pads and dropped on to the dirt.

"Catch the ball with your hands, not

your chest." Coach shouted. "Jamar, show Campbell how to hold his hands."

Jamar pulled Leo out of line and formed a kind of circle of his hands with his thumbs overlapping and his pointer fingers touching. Leo stared at the sophomore's large, strong hands as Jamar explained, "You want the tip of the ball to go into the circle. That way you have both hands on the ball and away from your pads."

"What if the ball isn't near your hands?" Leo asked.

He could tell Jamar was smiling under his helmet. "Then you got to adjust," he said. "Believe me, the JV quarterbacks aren't like Mahomes and Herbert. You got to do a lot of adjusting."

Leo nodded. Jamar eyed Leo's bare hands. "You might want to get some receiver's gloves," he said as he held up his gloved hands. "They got a whole bunch down at Muzinsky's. They'll help you catch the ball."

Practice continued with the receivers running patterns and the quarterbacks throwing passes. Jamar was right. Some passes were low and others sailed over Leo's head.

On one pattern the ball was high again, but Leo jumped, got his left hand on the ball, and pulled it in as he tumbled to the ground.

"Great catch! Great effort!" Coach K. shouted. "That's how you help your quarterback."

Another pass over the middle was right on Leo's numbers, but he took his eyes off the ball at the last second and it bounced off his hands.

"Get the ball first," Coach reminded Leo. "Watch it right into your hands . . . every time."

Leo slapped his thigh and scolded himself silently as he got back in line. *You're not going to make wide receiver if you keep dropping passes.*

An hour later, Leo walked back to the locker room with Hank and Sebby. "How did it go with you guys?" he asked.

"Okay," Hank said. "There's a lot to learn. It's more complicated than playing flag football at Sligo."

Sebby agreed. "Coach keeps telling us to stay in our lane. Do the assignment. I guess you can't just run around and tackle people."

"Too bad for you," Hank laughed. "That's what you like about football."

Leo pulled out the passing tree to show his friends. "We've got to learn these patterns. Coach said there may be more." He looked at Hank. "Do you think they'll put you on offense or defense?"

"Offense. They always need offensive linemen, and I'm big enough. What about you, Sebby?"

"Defense. Not many guys want to play linebacker. How about the wide receivers?"

"Looks like lots of guys want to play the position," Leo said.

Hank nodded. "I guess everyone wants to score touchdowns."

Chapter
THREE

Leo took out his phone and texted Hank, Sebby, and Ginny.

meet me at sligo in 20 – got something to show you – i'll bring a football

Leo's phone pinged three times within the next minute with several thumbs-up from his friends. He grabbed a football and a bag from Muzinsky's Sports Shop and headed out the door.

Standing in the Saturday sunshine, Leo saw his friends coming down the slope leading to Sligo Park.

"So, what's this thing you want to show us?" Hank asked.

Leo flipped the football to Ginny and reached into the bag. He brought out two black-and-silver receiver's gloves and put them on. Then he held his palms out to show his friends.

"Cool," Ginny said.

"When did you get them?" Sebby asked.

"First thing this morning. I figured I was dropping too many passes at tryouts this week, and I thought these might help."

"I noticed Jamar wears them," Hank said. "But his are red. I like the black-and-silver better."

Leo nodded. "Yeah, he told me I should get them." Leo started jogging toward the open field. "Come on, let's run some pass patterns."

Ginny tossed the football to Leo, who grabbed it and tucked it under his arm.

"Hey, the gloves work!" Sebby teased. "You didn't drop it."

Leo made a face at Sebby. He knew his friend was just joking, but still . . . he didn't like it. Leo pointed around the field with the football.

"I'll run patterns. Ginny, you play defensive back and try to cover me."

"What about me?" Sebby protested. "I can cover you."

"She's faster," Leo said.

Ginny smiled and shrugged. "He has a point."

"Sebby, you and Hank can trade off throwing passes," Leo continued. "The guy who isn't throwing can count to three Mississippi. The quarterback has to throw by three Mississippi."

"I'll take the first turn at quarterback," Hank declared. Leo and Hank huddled together.

"What do you want to run?" Hank asked Leo.

"Why don't we start with a down and in?" Leo whispered, and lined up to the right of his quarterback.

Ginny took her stance a few yards away from Leo. "Let's see if those gloves make you into a real pass catcher," she said with a small smile.

Sebby hiked the ball and started the count.

"One Mississippi..."

Leo dashed straight down the field, leaned right, and then broke sharply to the left.

"Two Mississippi..."

The ball was in the air and a half step behind Leo. He reached back with his gloved hands, but the ball bounced off his hip.

"Incomplete pass," Ginny called out.

"My bad," Hank said, tapping his chest.

Leo shook his head. "I should have had it. I got my hands on it."

"You mean you got your gloves on it," Sebby corrected as he spun the ball in his hands.

"I'll run a deep slant," Leo whispered to Hank for the next play.

Leo took off, running right at Ginny.

"One Mississippi..."

At the last moment, he angled toward the middle of the field.

"Two Mississippi..."

Ginny could not react in time as Leo sped by her and into the open. Hank's pass was right on target. Leo gathered it in at full stride and kept running.

"Touchdown!" he shouted.

Leo kept running patterns. Down and outs. Hook and goes. Quick slants. The whole passing tree.

Sebby switched with Hank at quarterback. The linebacker's passes were more scattershot than Hank's throws. Sebby also insisted he trade places with Ginny at cornerback.

"No way you can cover Leo," Ginny said. "He's too fast for you."

"Don't worry, I'll cover him."

Leo held up his hands when the two switched. "Remember, we're playing touch football. You're not supposed to tackle me."

But Ginny was right. Leo had too much speed for Sebby. After a few passes, Sebby surrendered and switched back.

"Last pass," Ginny called out after about a half hour. "This defensive back is getting tired."

"Let's try that deep slant again," Hank suggested. Leo nodded, then jogged out to his position and stood with his gloved hands on his hips.

Sebby hiked the ball and started the count.

"One Mississippi . . . two Mississippi . . . three Mississippi."

Leo was a step or two past Ginny when he looked back for the ball. Hank's pass was perfect, but the ball bounced off Leo's gloves and fell to the grass.

"Arrrrrrgh!" Leo cried out to the sky. "I cannot believe I dropped that one. It was right in my hands."

Leo turned to Ginny. "Come on, one more pass," he begged.

"No way. We said that was the last one."

Leo's shoulders slumped. He walked slowly back to where Sebby and Hank were standing. Sebby put his arm around Leo's shoulder.

"I don't think it's the gloves," he said.

Chapter
Four

Leo bounded down the stairs and into the kitchen. His mother and father were sitting at the table staring at their laptops. Mr. and Mrs. Campbell were child psychologists who helped kids with their problems.

"Have you finished your homework?" Mom asked.

"Yup."

"Did you study for your American history quiz?"

"No worries."

"What is the quiz on?" Dad asked.

"The American Revolution."

Leo's parents started to pepper him with questions about the long-ago conflict.

"What was the first battle in the war?"

"Lexington and Concord."

"Who was the commander of the British troops when they captured New York City?"

"William Howe. His brother Richard was an admiral for the British."

"What year was the Battle of Saratoga?"

"Seventeen seventy-seven, and there were two battles."

"Why were the Battles of Saratoga important?"

"It was a big win for the American Continental army and helped convince the French and Spanish governments to send aid to the colonists."

Leo's dad looked over at his wife. "Sounds like he knows his stuff."

"That's why I don't want him to play tackle football," she said as she turned her attention back to her computer. "He may injure that wonderful brain."

Leo rolled his eyes. His parents had had this discussion many times before.

"That usually only happens to guys who play for a long time," Dad said, then looked at his son. "Leo will probably just play for a few years in high school . . . like I did."

"I don't know," Mom said as she closed her laptop. "He could still get hurt. High school kids get concussions too."

"That's why I only played flag during elementary and middle school," Leo said.

"You could still play flag," Mom insisted. "Isn't there a boys' team at the high school?"

"Yeah, but it's not the same," Leo said. "Football is a big deal at Newport High. Hank and Sebby are playing tackle."

Mom didn't answer. She got up and went into the living room, then started to play the piano that stood in the corner. A beautiful tune filled the house.

"That's nice," Dad said, trying to break the tension. "What song is it?"

"'I'll Never Go There Anymore,'" Mom said as she kept playing. "Bill Charlap played it on one of his early albums. I think his father wrote it."

Mom began another song and Dad turned to Leo. "When's the first game?"

"I'll text you the schedule," Leo said as

they grabbed their phones. Leo got up and stood behind his father as the Newport High School junior varsity football schedule appeared on his screen.

Newport High School
Junior Varsity Football Schedule
All games are on Thursdays at 3:30 p.m.

September 24	Manchester HS
October 1	at Riverside HS
October 8	Marshall HS
October 15	at Jackson HS
October 22	at Milford HS
October 29	Fairport HS
November 5	at Clinton HS
November 12	Kingston HS

"The first game is a week from Thursday against Manchester High. We play eight straight Thursday games until the second week of November."

"You don't play Webster High School? I thought they were your biggest rival?"

"No, only the varsity plays them."

"How have the practices been going?" Dad asked in a soft voice, hoping Mom would not hear him over the piano music.

Leo thought back over the past two weeks. The heat, the sweat, the endless exercises and drills. The plays and patterns he had to learn. The fingertip catches and dropped passes. Too many dropped passes.

"Okay, I guess," Leo said. "Before tomorrow's practice, Coach is going to post lists outside the gym saying who is going to play what position."

"Do you think he will pick you to play wide receiver?"

"I don't know. There are some sophomores, like Jamar Johnson, who played wide receiver last season." Leo paused and then finally admitted something he had been thinking for days. "They are bigger than me and just as fast. . . . My guess is that Coach will probably pick them as the starters."

"Maybe he will pick you as a sub or a backup," Dad suggested.

Leo didn't say anything. He did not want to get stuck on defense or, even worse, special teams.

"How about Hank and Sebastian? Where

do you think Coach will put them?"

"Hank is pretty much a sure thing for offensive line and Sebby will probably play on defense." He smiled when he thought of his friends. "They don't care about scoring touchdowns—they just like hitting people."

Dad stood up. "Well, wherever Coach puts you, just give it all you got. That's what makes football such a great game. You need a lot of different players—linemen, running backs, and even special team guys—to have a good team."

Leo sat for a while and listened to the music. He understood what his father was saying, but he was not sure he wanted to believe it.

Chapter
FIVE

There was a crowd around the wall outside the boys' locker room when Leo, Hank, and Sebby arrived before practice. Approaching the wall, Leo felt a bit out of breath even though he had not been running. Leo saw the long lists of names when he got closer.

OFFENSE	DEFENSE	SPECIAL TEAMS
Randy Bevins	Alex Archer	Dallas Traylor
Jack Leekley	Luis Castro	Ed Silbert
Jamar Johnson	Leo Campbell	Lester Goldberg
J. P. Hamilton	Paul Zagaeski	Joseph Lovano
Hank Harris	Sebastian Bates	Mike Lane
Jake Healy	Gavin Teis	Kobe Jackson

His name was near the top of the list . . . for defense. Leo checked the offense list for wide receivers.

"J. P. Hamilton made offense," he said to Hank in a low voice. "I thought I was a better wide receiver than he was."

"They put you on defense," Hank said. "Maybe it's like Ginny told you. You might be a really good defensive back."

Leo eyed the lists. "That's easy for you to say. You made offense."

Hank laughed as he turned away from the wall. "Yeah, offensive line is the real glamour position. I'll probably score a million touchdowns. Face it, the only time offensive linemen get noticed is when they are called for a holding penalty."

"Come on, I'm on defense with you," Sebby said, pointing at his name on the defense list. "Coach made his decisions. Now we have to learn how to get better at our positions."

The rest of the practice was Leo learning how to play defensive back. For the first drill, Coach K. set out a series of orange plastic cones.

"This will help you with your quickness," he said.

Each of the new defenders backpedaled five yards from the first cone. When Coach shouted, "Go," the defensive back dug his foot in the dirt and burst forward five yards on an angle to another orange cone. They repeated this action two more times before Coach said, "Go long!" and tossed them the football so they could "make a play on the ball."

In the next drill, each defensive back ran sideways along a yard line facing the right. When Coach called out, "Switch," the defensive back had to turn his hips so he was facing left.

"This will help you stay with the receiver when he cuts or makes a move," Coach explained. "A defensive back has to be able to turn on a dime."

At first Leo felt strange running backward and sideways. Sometimes his feet got tangled. Once he even tumbled to the turf. But after a few of the drills, it started to feel all right. Almost natural. He even got Coach to shout out, "Good work, Campbell. That's how to move your feet."

In the next drill, Coach tossed up a football between two defensive backs to see who would come down with the ball. Coach kept up his chatter as the players tangled to get the ball.

"Make sure if you don't get the ball, the other guy doesn't either. Get your hands into his hands. Remember, it's a fight; you have to win it."

Finally, Coach gave the players some tips about recognizing the wide receiver's routes. He looked at the group and settled his eyes on Leo. "Some of you guys tried out for wide receiver, so you remember that passing tree."

Leo and the other defensive backs nodded their helmets. It seemed like most of the Raiders' defensive backs were guys who had wanted to be on offense.

"Good," Coach continued. "Because the wide receivers will be running those routes." He held up the football and moved it around as if to emphasize his point. "If you can anticipate where the receiver is going, you may stop him or even better, make the quarterback decide not to throw him the ball."

After more drills, Coach K. and Coach Carter brought the quarterbacks, wide receivers, and defensive backs together. "Let's see how you guys do against one another. Wide receivers line up at the right and left ends. Defensive backs cover man-to-man. Quarterbacks switch every five passes. Let's go."

Leo stood waiting his turn and thinking, *If I can make the receivers look bad, maybe Coach Carter will give me another chance to play on offense.*

Soon the warm September air was filled with footballs and Coach K.'s instructions.

"Move your feet. . . . Make that cut quicker. . . . Go for the ball. . . . Watch the receiver's hips, not his head. . . . Get your hands up. . . . Break hard to the ball."

On one pattern late in the practice, Jamar faked a down and out and went long. Leo sensed the pattern and did not fall for the fake. He switched the position of his hips like he had in the earlier drill and ran step-for-step with the sophomore receiver.

The pass was right on target. Leo looked back and saw the ball out of the corner of his eye. Jamar had his hands up, ready to make the catch. Leo stretched out his left hand so it was between Jamar's arms. The ball bounced off both their hands and onto the ground.

Jamar lost his balance and tumbled to the dirt, dragging Leo with him.

"Great play!" Coach K. shouted. "That's how you get your hands in there."

Leo reached out his gloved hand and pulled Jamar to his feet. "Nice play," Jamar said. "I thought I had you beat."

Leo dusted himself off and jogged back to the line of defensive backs. Coach Carter stood with his hands on his hips and a wide smile on his face. "We may have found ourselves a cover corner," he said, looking straight at Leo.

Chapter SIX

The Newport High School JV football team burst out of the locker room, their metal cleats clattering against the roadway leading to the high school field. The Raiders were ready for their first game.

Standing shoulder-to-shoulder with his teammates, Leo could feel the excitement of the players. His heart was pumping in his chest.

He glanced over to Hank. "Real football," he said, smiling under his red helmet.

"Real football," Hank repeated.

Coach called the defense together. He named the game's starters, including Sebby at linebacker and Leo at cornerback. The players circled and pressed in toward their coach as he gave them their final instructions.

"We're going to give up some yardage today. This isn't baseball. You can't pitch a no-hitter in football. The key is not to give up any big plays. Hard work on three."

The players put their hands in the middle of the circle and counted off, "One . . . two . . . three . . ." and then shouted, "Hard work!"

The Raiders and the Manchester High School Lancers were almost pitching no-hitters early in the game. The offenses struggled to get any momentum. The game remained in the middle of the field with lots of punts and stalled drives.

In the second quarter, the Lancers' quarterback faded back for a pass. Covering the left end, Leo backpedaled with the Lancers' wide receiver. When Leo saw him dig in his right foot and cut to the sideline, Leo thought, *He's doing a down and out!*

The ball was already in the air as Leo darted toward it. *I can pick this one off!* Leo thought as he reached for the football.

But he was a split second too late, and the

ball whizzed past the very edge of his fingertips. The Lancers' receiver bobbled the ball for an instant but gathered it in and headed up the sideline, with Leo five yards behind.

The receiver dodged a tackle by the Raiders' safety by angling to the middle of the field and pulling away from Leo.

Touchdown! And just the kind of big play Coach did not want the defense to give up. Manchester added a two-point conversion on a run up the middle. The Lancers were ahead 8–0.

Coach stepped up to Leo as the defense came off the field. "Remember," he said in a calm but firm voice, "don't go for the ball unless you are one hundred percent sure you can get it. Just tackle him or push him out of bounds. I would rather give up a first down than a big play."

Leo looked at the ground. Coach tapped him on the helmet. "Okay, head up. Do your job. Make the next play."

Leo plopped himself on the bench, tilting his helmet back on his head. "Shake it off," Sebby said, standing above him. "There's a lot of football left."

The Lancers' big play seemed to wake up Newport's offense. The Raiders moved down the field with a mix of runs and short passes. Just before the half ended, Jake Healy, the Raiders' running back, bolted through the right side behind a big block by Hank to score on a twelve-yard run.

But the Raiders missed the two-point conversion and so trailed 8–6 at the half.

Newport kept the momentum as Jake returned the second-half kickoff to midfield. The Raiders' offense drove downfield until they were right on the Lancers' goal line. Randy Bevins, the Raiders' starting quarterback, scored on a quarterback sneak.

The Raiders missed on the extra points when Jamar couldn't hold on to a short pass. Newport led 12–8.

After the Raiders' second score, the two offenses kept stalling as the game moved into the fourth and final quarter.

Manchester got the ball at their own 30-yard line with four minutes to go in the game. The Lancers began to drive downfield as the seconds ticked away. But the drive began to stall at the Raiders' 20-yard line.

"Come on," shouted Sebby to his tired teammates in the defensive huddle. "We need a stop."

Sensing Manchester might go in for the winning score, the crowd scattered around the Newport High School stadium began to chant.

"DEFENSE...DEFENSE...DEFENSE!"

Leo looked at the scoreboard.

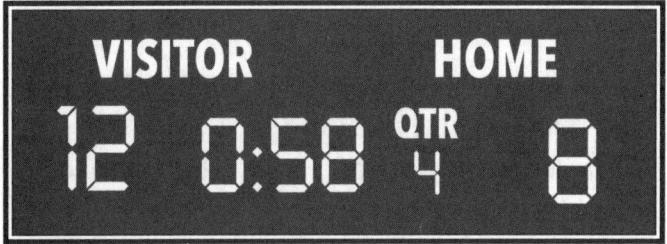

It was fourth down and five yards to go at the 20-yard line, less than a minute to play. The Lancers had one more down to keep their chances alive.

"Ready ... set ... hut one ..." The Manchester quarterback spun and pitched the ball to his halfback on a sweep play.

They're coming my way! Leo thought, and

reacted quickly, slipping by the wide receiver who was trying to block him. He put his shoulder into the runner's churning upper legs but felt him slipping away.

Just then Sebby came crashing in, sending both Leo and the ball carrier to the ground. Leo looked at the first down marker on the sideline.

The runner was two yards short of a first down. The defense had made a stop. It was Newport's ball.

The Raiders ran out the clock as Randy "took a knee" on three straight plays. The Newport JV had hung on to a 12–8 win.

Back in the locker room, the team celebrated. Leo looked down the benches and saw the team's starting halfback sitting back with his ankle raised and packed in ice bags.

"What's with Jake?" Leo asked.

"He twisted his ankle really bad on one of the last plays of the game," Hank explained. "The trainer doesn't think anything is broken, but he'll be out for at least a few weeks."

Sebby pulled his shoulder pads over his

head. "Guess we will need a new running back."

"And kick returner," Leo added. "Remember Jake has been returning kickoffs . . . punts too."

Hank inspected a bruise that was popping up on his forearm. "Maybe you should try out for that kick returner job," he said to Leo. "It might give you a chance to score a touchdown."

CHAPTER
SEVEN

Leo stood on the Newport practice field and stared up into the clear September sky as the football spun his way. He caught the ball just as several players whooshed by him.

Their speed made Leo almost jump. *Whoa,* he thought. *What if those guys had hit me? This kick returning may be trickier—and more dangerous—than I'd thought.*

"Scared you, didn't I?" Sebby said as he walked back past Leo.

Coach K. blew his whistle. "You may want to signal for a fair catch," he said to Leo. Then he started waving his left hand above his head and added, "By waving your hand like this, especially when the kicks are high or short."

Coach continued talking. "But don't worry. This isn't like the NFL, where the punters kick the ball a mile high and the kickers boot every kickoff through the end zone. You'll get plenty of chances to run back kicks."

That's exactly what was beginning to worry Leo.

For the rest of the practice, Coach showed Leo and the two other Raiders who were trying out for Jake's position what it took to be a kick returner on special teams.

Coach gathered the boys together. "Remember, you want to secure the football," he said as he acted out catching the ball and tucking it under his arm. "That's the most important thing. I would rather have no gain on the return than to cough up a fumble."

He took a few steps forward. "Once you have the football, look downfield and quickly check out the defense. Look for any openings or places where we have blockers. Then move decisively . . . don't hesitate. I want you running north and south, not east and west."

"North and south?" one of the other players asked, sounding confused.

"I want you running downfield, not across the field." Coach tossed the ball up and down a few times, adding, "We won't run it back all the way every time, but we want to make some positive yardage whenever we can."

Leo nodded. It sounded like running back kicks was going to be a tough way to score touchdowns.

The practice continued. Leo and the others fielded kick after kick. Coach K. was right; most were low enough that they could be returned. Leo also was finding that for some reason, he was better at catching punts and kickoffs than passes.

Late in the afternoon, as the sun was beginning to slip behind the trees on the edge of the field, the Raiders' punter boomed out a long kick. Leo drifted back and caught the ball. He looked up and saw the bunches of special teams players racing his way. Leo took a couple quick steps to his right, saw an opening, and dug his cleats into the dirt and cut sharply to his left, heading downfield.

The special teams players' momentum carried them past Leo, who raced untouched down the middle of the field.

Coach blew his whistle. "Great job!" he shouted. "Leo got the ball, checked the field, and made a quick, decisive move. No hesitation . . . that's how we do it."

Coach waved his clipboard above his head to bring the punter, the kick returners, and the special teams players in. Leo looked around at the other kick return candidates and wondered who Coach would pick for the job.

"Listen up," Coach said as he checked the notes he had on his clipboard. "Everyone did a good job, but I am going to recommend to Coach Carter that Leo be our main kick returner in our game on Thursday against Riverside. But we may use Dallas too."

"All three of you will keep practicing with the special teams," he added. "Campbell will keep practicing with the defense."

Leo felt a sweet feeling of satisfaction sweep over him. He had won the kick returning job. At least for now. Maybe now he would get a real chance to score a touchdown. Starting on Thursday.

As he walked off the practice field, Hank and Sebby caught up with him. "How did it go?" Hank asked.

"Coach is going to let me run back kicks," Leo said as he pulled off his helmet and shook the sweat from his head. "But he may give Dallas a chance too."

"Did you drop any of the kicks?" Sebby asked.

"I don't think I bobbled a single one," Leo said, and held up his gloved hands. "Maybe it's the gloves."

"So, you're a special teams guy now," Hank said, clapping Leo on the shoulder pads.

"Coach has been using you guys on special teams. How do you like it?"

"Fine with me," Hank said. "Special teams need blockers too."

"Yeah," Sebby agreed. "I'm down with

anything to get me more playing time. Anyway, special teams are still part of the team."

Leo stepped into the locker room. "Looks like I'm going to find out."

CHAPTER
EIGHT

Leo stretched out on the sofa in the den of his house. He was reading a history of the NFL called *Gridiron: Stories from 100 Years of the National Football League* for the second time.

He could hear his mother playing the piano in the living room. Leo recognized the playful Duke Ellington tune and started to hum the song. At the end he even sang a few of the words of "Don't Get Around Much Anymore" softly to himself.

Dad poked his head into the den. "There you are," he said. "What are you doing?"

Leo held up the book. "Just reading."

"I'm all for that," Dad said with a quick nod. "How's the book?"

"Good. I've read it before. Did you know it only cost teams a hundred bucks to join the NFL when it started?"

"A hundred bucks? Now NFL franchises are worth billions."

"Yeah, and a guy named George Halas, who was at the meeting to set up the league, claimed nobody paid the money. He said the ten guys in the room probably didn't have a hundred bucks among them."

Dad sat down. "How's practice going? Did you try out for kick returner?"

Leo closed the book and sat up. He could tell his father wanted to talk some football. "Yeah, it looks like I'll get a chance to run some kicks back."

"Great. I guess you've changed your mind about special teams."

"Kind of," Leo admitted. "But returning kicks is not the same as being a wide receiver. I mean, receivers score a lot more TDs than kick returners."

"Don't be so sure. Special teams can make a big difference in a football game." Dad left the room and came back with his laptop, then sat down again and propped it on his thighs. His fingers moved quickly across the keyboard. "I think I'll look up who holds the record for most non-offensive touchdowns."

"Non-offensive touchdowns?" Leo asked. He had never heard that term.

"You know, like kickoff or punt returns, pick-six interceptions or fumble returns. Non-offensive touchdowns are just plays where the other team starts off with the ball but your team scores."

Dad kept typing away and staring at the screen. "I wonder if Pro Football Reference has a category for that?"

Leo got up and knelt by his father's chair to look at the screen.

"Yeah, here it is. Non-offensive touchdowns career," Dad said, and clicked a few more keys. A row of pictures of football players appeared. Below the pictures there was a list of the players' names and the number of non-offensive touchdowns they had scored.

PLAYER	N-OTD	YEARS
Devin Hester	20	2006-2016
Deion Sanders	19	1989-2005
Ron Woodson	17	1987-2003
Ronde Barber	14	1997-2012
Brian Mitchell	13	1990-2003

"Devin Hester," Dad declared, pointing to the name at the top of the list. "Twenty career non-offensive touchdowns."

"Devin Hester?" Leo repeated. "I've never heard of him."

"He played for the Bears years ago. Let's look up his stats." A few keystrokes revealed a row of numbers.

DEVIN HESTER

	Punt Returns			Kickoff Returns		
	Rets	Yds	TDs	Rets	Yds	TDs
2006	47	600	3	20	528	2
2007	42	651	4	43	934	2

"Whoa, look at this," Dad said, pointing at the screen. "Hester scored touchdowns on fourteen punt returns and five kickoff returns during his career."

Leo's eyes took in the numbers. "He scored twelve TDs on kick returns in his first two seasons." Leo leaned back. "That's unbelievable."

"He even returned a missed field goal for a touchdown in his first season," Dad noted. "That's how he got up to twenty non-offensive touchdowns."

Leo kept studying the numbers. "Looks like he didn't score as often after the first two seasons."

"They probably started kicking the ball away from him," Dad suggested.

"I would kick the ball out of bounds instead of kicking it to that guy," Leo said. Then he saw something else. "Hey, Hester started out as a defensive back."

"Like someone else I know," Dad said.

"Anybody else score a lot of non-offensive touchdowns?" Leo asked.

Dad clicked back to the list. "Deion Sanders

had nineteen," he said.

"I've heard of him. Prime Time," Leo said. "He's coaching in college now."

Dad clicked on to Sanders' stats again, pointing at the dozens of numbers on the screen.

"He returned nine interceptions for touchdowns. Six punt returns, three kickoffs, and one fumble recovery. There are a lot of ways to score touchdowns in a football game."

"And it looks like Prime Time found almost every one," Leo laughed.

Dad went back to his laptop. "Let's see if we can find some Devin Hester highlights on YouTube."

Leo leaned in closer as film from long-ago football games flashed across the screen. Hester running back kicks. Dodging tacklers. Leaving them in his dust. Racing down the sideline and into the end zone. Time after time after time.

Leo sat transfixed by the Hester highlights. And with the piano music drifting in from the living room, he started dreaming of scoring touchdowns again.

CHAPTER
NINE

The Newport captains ran back from the coin flip at midfield that began the Riverside game. "We're receiving," they said.

Coach K. turned and called out, "Kickoff return team, get out there. Leo, you are back in single safety."

Leo snapped his chin strap and ran out to the 10-yard line. He took a deep breath and wiped his sweating palms against his football pants.

The Riverside kickoff was low, bouncing just beyond the 20-yard line. Leo glanced up the field just as the ball, tumbling wildly, was about to settle in his arms. The ball bounced off his chest and spun to the ground.

Oh no, a fumble on my first kickoff!

By the time Leo grabbed the ball, the Rams' defense was all around him, and they drove him to the ground. He had barely gained a yard.

Coach K. met him at the sidelines holding up one finger. "Remember, the first rule of kick returning is to secure the ball."

Leo could feel his chin drop. Coach tapped his helmet. "Shake it off," he said. "Play good defense. You'll get the next kick."

The Raiders' offense went "three and out," punting after three plays gained almost no yardage. The Rams took over with good field position near midfield.

The Riverside Rams were not much of a passing team. Instead, they ran the ball into the middle of the Newport defense play after play, trying to wear the Raiders' defense down.

After three first downs, the Raiders' defense stiffened. It was third down with two yards to go at the 20-yard line. Leo and the other defensive backs pressed closer to the middle of the line, expecting another run.

The Rams' quarterback faked a handoff to the fullback and then spun to pitch the ball to his halfback, sweeping around the left end.

Leo fell for the fake but quickly recovered, racing after the halfback. He leaped and tripped up the halfback, but not before he had gained eight yards and another first down.

"Great play," Sebby said in the huddle. "You saved us a touchdown."

Leo's hustle did not save a touchdown for long. After three more runs, the Rams' fullback slammed into the end zone for the first touchdown. Riverside added the extra point with a kick right through the uprights.

Riverside led 7–0.

"Leo, you are back receiving again," Coach K. shouted. "Remember, get the ball first!"

The ball bounced in front of Leo again. But this time he hooked it into his hands and then started upfield. Leo had gone about twenty yards when a Ram defender jolted him with a hard tackle. Leo hit the ground but held on to the ball.

Coach K. was clapping as the kickoff team and Leo jogged to the sidelines. "Good job. You gave us decent field position."

"You okay?" Sebby asked as he slid next to Leo on the bench. "You took a major hit."

"Yeah, no worries," Leo responded, although he could still feel the hit in his chest.

The Raiders' offense finally got going. After a couple quick first downs, Randy faked a handoff to the fullback, took two quick steps back, and hit Jamar on a deep slant over the middle. The wide receiver took the pass in stride, avoided one tackler, and took it all the way to the end zone.

Touchdown!

The Raiders scored a two-point conversion on a quarterback draw and so took an 8–7 lead into halftime.

In the second half, the Raiders' defense "packed the box," pulling the safeties and defensive backs closer to the defensive line to stop the Rams runners and force the Rams to pass. The strategy worked and the Rams had to punt.

The first kick was high and short. Leo signaled for a fair catch by waving his left hand in the air. Later, the Rams' second punt was low, so Leo caught it on the run, slipped by the first tackler, and raced up the sideline. He had gained around twenty-five yards before a Ram defender pushed him out of bounds.

Leo skidded across the sideline dirt but popped up happy. Sebby and Hank, who had been blocking on the return, were among the teammates slapping Leo on his shoulder pads and helmet.

"Way to go."

"Great runback."

"You took it past midfield."

Because the Raiders had good field position, the offense only had to drive another forty yards for a touchdown. The touchdown and two-point conversion put the Raiders ahead 16–7.

The coaches were roaming up and down the sidelines, telling the defense, "No big plays. . . . No big plays."

The Rams quarterback finally completed a few short passes, but Leo and the other defensive backs were ready. They tackled the wide receivers before they could turn upfield and held them to short gains.

The Raiders' offense tacked on another score late in the fourth quarter, when Jamar caught a long pass. The score put the game away, 22–7.

Coach Carter was pumped up after the win. "That was a total team win. Everybody helped today," he said to the Raiders. "Offense . . . defense . . . special teams."

Coach K. was happy too. He grabbed Leo as he was walking off the field with his helmet on his hip and a big smile.

"You did a good job returning kicks today," he said, and pulled out a tablet to show Leo his game stats.

Kick Returns	Number	Yards	Average	TDs
Kickoff	2	22	11.0	0
Punts	2	33	16.5	0

"You'll be returning kicks until Jake gets back from his ankle injury," Coach continued.

"Great!" Leo shouted, and started to walk away. He could almost feel himself crossing the goal line.

Coach K. grabbed him by his shoulder pads. "As long as you can keep it up."

Chapter
TEN

"When does the game start?" Leo asked as he and Sebby and Hank walked quickly to the high school football stadium. It was a cool, cloudy October Sunday, and the boys were heading to the girls' flag football game.

"One o'clock," Hank said.

"Who are they playing?"

"Marshall."

"They any good?"

"I don't know." Hank smiled and added, "I forgot to check the betting line."

Sebby piped up. "I can't imagine they have anyone as good as Ginny."

The three friends stopped and stood outside the high school gym, where the schedules of the fall sports teams and the results of the games were posted. They studied the Newport JV football schedule.

September 24	Manchester HS	W 16–12
October 1	at Riverside HS	W 22–7
October 8	Marshall HS	W 26–6
October 15	at Jackson HS	W 30–12
October 22	at Milford HS	L 20–8
October 29	Fairport HS	W 18–14
November 5	Clinton HS	
November 12	Kingston HS	
July 21	American Legion Post 268 Yankees	

"Five wins and one loss," Leo said. "That's not too bad."

"I thought we could have beat Milford," Sebby said, still studying the schedule.

"They were pretty good," Hank said.

Sebby pointed at the wall. "Check out the girls' flag football team. They've got a winning record too."

"And it looks as if they're scoring like

crazy," Leo said, turning away from the wall. "Come on, let's go. It's almost one o'clock."

The boys took their seats among the small crowd of parents and students just as Marshall kicked off. A Newport player gathered the ball at the 20-yard line and pitched it back to Ginny, who scampered another thirty yards before a defender grabbed her flag.

"That was a smart play to get the ball to Ginny," Leo observed.

"Yeah, she looks like a good kick returner," Hank said, and turned to Leo. "Watch out—she might take your job!"

"I've been doing all right," Leo replied, and then shook his head. "I thought I was going to take that punt against Jackson back all the way."

"Yeah, that guy just tripped you up at the last second." The boys looked back toward the field.

Just about every play in the Raiders' offense was designed to get the ball to Ginny. She caught passes, and took pitchouts for sweeps and handoffs for runs and reverses as the Newport offense moved down the field for its first score. On a short pass to Ginny.

On defense, Ginny played safety but came up quickly on running plays to make the stops.

Hank leaned back in amazement. "Man, Ginny is doing everything."

"She's all over the field," Sebby agreed.

"Maybe we should have stayed with flag football," Leo said as Ginny weaved through the Marshall defense for another long run. "She looks like she's having all the fun."

Sebby shook his head firmly. "No way. We're all starting and playing for a team with a winning record. That's pretty cool if you ask me."

"Yeah, but look at Ginny," Leo said, motioning to the field. "She's scoring like two or three touchdowns a game. I think that's even cooler if you ask me."

"You're a kick returner," Sebby argued. "You got a chance to score."

"Especially with Sebby and me blocking for you," Hank said. "And you got a chance for a pick-six if you intercept a pass. Who's that guy for the Cowboys who had a bunch of pick-six TDs?"

"DaRon Bland."

"Yeah, but it's still not like being a wide receiver," Leo said, and then pointed down to the field. "Or being like Ginny."

The three teammates settled in to watch the game. Newport was having an easy time of it with Marshall. By halftime Ginny had scored three touchdowns and the Raiders led, 20–0.

"Ginny is a one-man team," Leo said at the half.

"One-woman team," Hank corrected.

"It's not just Ginny," Sebby said. "Abby Bannister is doing a good job at quarterback."

"Abigail Bannister," Hank corrected his friend again.

"What are you talking about?" Leo asked.

"She told me in biology she wants to be called Abigail. She says there are too many Abbys in our class."

"Whatever."

At the beginning of the second half, Marshall started to put together a drive with a mix of runs, reverses, and short passes. Within minutes Marshall had the ball on the 16-yard line.

"If they can get a touchdown," Leo said.

"They could make a game of it." Hank and Sebby nodded and leaned forward on their stadium seats.

The Marshall quarterback faked a hand-off, looked to her left, and tossed a pass toward the sideline. The pass floated a bit too much. Sensing the play, Ginny darted from the defensive backfield, grabbed the ball, and took off down the sideline.

The boys jumped to their feet along with the rest of the crowd and pumped fists into the air as Ginny raced for another touchdown. They traded high fives as she crossed the goal line.

"Eighty-four yards!"

"She's got four touchdowns!"

"That girl can flat-out *play*."

They finally sat down. "See?" Hank said, elbowing Leo. "You can score a TD playing defense."

"But remember," Sebby warned, echoing the Raiders coaches. "Do your job first."

Chapter
ELEVEN

"Back . . . back . . . now make a play on the ball."

Leo grabbed the ball out of the air and tucked it under his arm. He took a few quick steps downfield.

The Raider defensive backs were doing the cone drill for what seemed to Leo to be the ten thousandth time that season. The weather was turning colder. A steamy September had slid into a chilly November. The sun was slipping lower in the sky.

"Good job, Leo," Coach K. said. "I like the way you keep your feet moving."

Coach was right. After weeks of practice and drills, the footwork and hip-twisting turns that had felt so strange weeks ago now seemed like second nature.

"Bring it in," Coach shouted. The defensive backs gathered around.

Leo looked at his teammates around the circle. *We've done a good job this season,* he thought. *Not too many big plays against us. But not many interceptions. I guess we are about even on winning the fifty-fifty balls. And we have been helping out against the run.*

But Coach K. wasn't about to hand out any compliments. "We got some tough games coming up," he declared. "Against some good wide receivers. This guy Corey Farr who plays for Clinton is the real deal."

Leo nodded. Clinton and Kingston high schools always had good football teams.

"The key is not giving up any big plays to these teams," Coach continued. "That means we have to tackle their wideouts and running backs right after they catch the ball. So let's go over the fundamentals of good tackling again."

Leo silently groaned to himself. He knew

Sebby loved all the hitting and tackling in football, but tackling was Leo's least favorite part of the game. He figured if he could break up the pass before the wide receiver could get his hands on the ball, he wouldn't have to tackle him. And that would be just fine.

And it would make his mom happy. If she had her way, Leo wouldn't hit anybody.

The players jogged over to a series of tackling dummies in a corner of the field. The defensive backs had nicknamed the heavy, black vinyl tackling dummies "Jefferson" after the great NFL wide receiver Justin Jefferson.

Coach stood near the dummies. "Let's go through the five elements of good tackling techniques. He held up one finger.

"One, eyes open, back straight.

"Two, keep your hands in tackling position." Coach held his hands out to the side and slightly in front of him.

"Three, keep your feet moving. Adjust your stance so your lead foot is the one closest to the ballcarrier.

"Four, drive into the ballcarrier with your shoulder." Coach took a quick step forward and leaned over as if he was about to make a tackle. "Keep your head to the ballcarrier's side. Do not . . . I repeat . . . *do not* lead with your helmet. Lead with your shoulder."

Finally, Coach held up all five fingers. "Five, wrap your arms around the ballcarrier."

Coach looked around the circle of players. There were no questions. The boys knew the tackling fundamentals and drill by heart.

"Okay, let's do it."

Leo and the other defensive backs threw themselves against the tackling dummies as Coach K. shouted out instructions: "Head up, don't look down. . . . Keep your feet moving. . . . Come on, Campbell, don't hold back. . . . Really drive forward into Jefferson. . . . The Clinton wide receivers aren't going to fall down by themselves. . . . You got to bring them down."

Leo was relieved when Coach K. called it quits after twenty bone-jarring minutes. "Okay, hit the showers."

Leo found Sebby and Hank as the team walked slowly toward the school. The field was almost dark. The lights from the school and the street cast a yellow glow over the players.

"I am beat," Leo complained. "Coach had us practicing tackling forever."

"You should have called me over," Sebby laughed. "I love hitting Jefferson."

"You better buckle your chin strap on Thursday," Hank advised. "That guy Corey Farr for Clinton is supposed to be good."

Leo wasn't so sure. "If he's so good, why isn't he on varsity?"

"Because Clinton always has really good teams."

"I don't know. . . . Coach makes him sound like the second coming of Jerry Rice or something."

"Maybe not Jerry Rice," Sebby teased. "But he could be the second Calvin Johnson."

"Megatron!" Hank shouted Johnson's nickname into the darkness. "I play him in *Madden NFL* all the time."

Sebby got serious for a moment. "If you can be the kind of cover corner who can take that guy Farr one-on-one for the whole game . . ."

"And not give up any big plays," Leo said, adding Coach K.'s favorite.

"It will really help the team," Sebby finished the thought.

"Will it help more than a pick-six?" Leo asked.

"Maybe not that much, but pretty close."

Chapter
TWELVE

"Which one is Corey Farr?" Leo asked as the Newport team went through their warm-up exercises.

"Number eighty," Sebby said, stretching his left leg.

80? I think that was Jerry Rice's number, Leo thought as he pumped his legs up and down. When he stopped, Leo searched the Clinton sideline of players. His eyes finally locked on the number 80.

"He doesn't look that tough," Leo said. But he could feel his voice tightening.

"That's not what I hear," Sebby said as he pounded Hank's shoulder pads. "You're going to have your hands full today."

The team huddled around Coach Carter.

"We're going to start with Leo trying to cover Number Eighty, Farr, one-on-one. Safeties, try to give him some help on the inside routes. And be sure to wrap him up quickly."

On the Clinton Cougars' first possession, Farr split out on the left side. Leo sized up his opposite number from across the line.

He's a little taller than me. Maybe a couple inches. And he's got those long arms and big hands. It's like he was born to be a wide receiver.

The Raiders stopped the Cougars' first two runs cold. Third and ten, and Leo lined up, ready for a pass. Sure enough, Farr dashed out five yards and then angled sharply toward the middle of the field. Leo couldn't stop him from catching the ball but tackled the Cougar wide receiver right away. Two yards short of the first down.

Leo felt good as he went back to receive the punt. The kick was short and Leo decided to let it hit the ground. The ball took a Cougar bounce that added about fifteen more yards to the kick.

Coach K. met Leo as the special team

came off the field. "Try to come up and fair catch a short kick like that." But then as Leo headed for the bench, he added, "Good tackle."

The game settled into a back-and-forth contest. Newport scored first on a twenty-two-yard touchdown pass that Jamar snagged in the corner of the end zone.

Clinton bounced back with a long drive that ended with a short run. Farr outleaped Leo to grab a high pass to add the two-point conversion.

The score was knotted at 8–8 at halftime.

If Leo had dreams of stopping Corey Farr, they hadn't come true. The rangy wide receiver was a big part of the Cougars' offense.

Farr caught several balls on down and ins, down and outs, and quick slants. There were no big plays, but Farr used his long arms and strong hands to hold on to the ball even when Leo was practically in his jersey.

The second half got off to a fast start when Leo took the ball at the 10-yard line and raced fifty yards up the right sideline behind a wall of blockers to the 40-yard line before he was pushed out of bounds.

With a short field, the Raiders drove all the way down near the Cougars' goal line, where the Clinton defense stiffened. It was fourth and goal at the 1-yard line when Randy, the Newport quarterback, called a time-out and walked to the sideline to talk to the coaches.

Leo turned to Sebby on the Raiders' bench. "I think they should run it right up the gut. Their defense is getting tired."

Sebby disagreed. "I say they should fake it and let Randy roll out. Then he can run or pass."

The defense and all the players on the bench stood up as the Raiders' quarterback returned to the field.

Sebby was right. Randy faked a handoff to the Raiders' fullback and rolled to his right. He tossed a short pass to the Raiders' tight end, who was wide-open at the back of the end zone.

Touchdown!

Clinton stopped the two-point try. Newport led 14–8.

The teams traded touchdowns, so Newport was still holding on to a 20–14 lead near the end of the fourth quarter.

The Clinton defense forced the Raiders to punt. The kick was a short one, and the Cougars took over at midfield with only three minutes to go.

The Raiders' defensive huddle filled with brave talk.

"Need a stop."

"Got to hold them."

"Dig in, guys."

Leo could feel his hands tingling as he lined up against Farr once again. He slapped his palms against the dirt and took a deep breath. He was ready.

Sure enough, the Clinton offense targeted Farr right away. A couple quick down and ins moved the ball to the 27-yard line.

The Cougars switched to the run. Two blasts into the line gained a total of seven tough yards. Now it was third and three on the 20-yard line with time ticking away.

Leo edged more to the middle of the field as he lined up against Farr again. *Got to take away that down-and-in pattern.*

Farr took three quick steps and broke to the left sideline. Leo stepped up, but Farr spun and broke downfield.

Oh no, he's going long!

Farr was two steps ahead with Leo racing to catch up. The Raiders' safety was moving over, but he was going to be too late.

Farr slowed slightly, and Leo turned his head to find the ball. It was falling fast, so Leo desperately reached and slapped the ball away just before Farr could grab it. Incomplete pass.

"Great play!" Sebby shouted above the cheering crowd.

A lucky play, Leo thought. *He had me beat.*

Coach Carter called time-out and brought the defense over to the sideline to huddle before the crucial fourth-down play.

"Let's double-team Farr on this play," he said. "Have the safety move over to help out Leo. Take that option away."

The Cougars tried a sweep instead. The Raiders stopped the running back a yard short of the first down. It was Newport's ball.

The Raiders ran out the clock and held on to their 20–14 win.

Coach K. found Leo as the players milled around the field, shaking one another's hands.

"Good work on Farr," Coach said, giving Leo a quick thumbs-up.

"How many passes did he catch?" Leo asked.

Coach turned his tablet around to show Leo the game statistics.

	Targets	Catches	Yards	TDs
Farr	12	9	101	0

"Nine catches for more than a hundred yards," Leo said, shaking his head. "That's a lot."

"Yeah, but remember he didn't make any big plays." Coach snapped the tablet shut and slapped Leo on the shoulder pads. "You did your job."

CHAPTER THIRTEEN

"How many more of these do I have to do?" Leo asked.

Mom looked into the bowl of carrot pieces that Leo had peeled and cut. "A couple more good-sized sticks should do it," she said.

Leo started peeling again. "Where's Dad?"

"He had a late appointment with a client. He said he'll be back in time for dinner."

Mom pointed at the carrot in Leo's hand. "Be careful with the knife," she said as Leo got ready to cut the carrot into smaller pieces.

"Don't worry, I will." Leo tossed the carrot pieces into the bowl when he finished.

"How's school going?" Mom asked.

"Okay. I'm getting all A's, except in French."

"*Pourquoi?*" Mom asked in French.

"*Je ne sais pas,*" Leo answered, keeping the French going. "*Je n'aime pas les langues,* I guess."

Mom smiled but dropped the French. "How's football going?"

"Okay."

Leo looked up from his kitchen work. "You should come to our next game. We're playing Kingston High. It's the last game of the season."

"I would worry too much," Mom said, shaking her head as she stirred a steaming pot at the stove. "I would hate to see you get hurt."

"I won't get hurt."

"You're a kick returner and defensive back, aren't you? Kick returners and defensive backs get hurt too."

"It's not that dangerous," Leo insisted. "When I'm returning kicks, I'm trying to make the other team miss me."

"And when you're a defensive back?" Mom asked.

"If I do my job right, the quarterback won't even throw the ball to the guy I'm covering."

Mom took the bowl with the carrot pieces and slid them into the boiling pot. "This has to cook for a while." She turned down the flame on the stove and set the timer.

She wandered into the living room, sat down at the piano, and started to play a slow song. Leo followed her into the room and sat in a chair near the piano.

"I still wish I could have played wide receiver this season," Leo said. "That would have been the best."

"Wide receivers get hurt," Mom said, still playing. "After all, they have the ball."

"Yeah, but . . ."

Mom looked up from the keys. "You know, sometimes you don't get to choose your talents."

"What do you mean?"

"Well, you wanted to be a wide receiver," Mom said as she switched to another tune. "But it seems like you are better at defensive back."

"And kick returns," Leo added.

Mom continued playing and talking. "When I was growing up, I wanted to be a concert pianist," she said, looking up and away from the piano. "I was even in the music program at Oberlin College."

"I'll bet you were really good," Leo said.

Mom smiled as she looked at Leo. "I *was* good," she said with a touch of sadness, and then added, "I was good enough to know I wasn't good enough.

"I switched schools and met your father," she said as she continued playing. "He was studying psychology. It seemed interesting and I was interested in him, so . . ."

"So you became a psychologist who helps kids," Leo said, completing her thought.

Mom nodded and started to play another song. Leo didn't recognize the tune.

"What is that one called?" he asked.

"'Nice Work If You Can Get It' by George Gershwin."

Leo was quiet as he listened to his mother play.

"It's not so bad," he said finally. "Kids need psychologists, and you still get to play the piano."

"Teams need defensive backs," Mom

answered, lifting her eyebrows a bit. "And you still get a chance to score touchdowns as a kick returner."

"Or as a defensive back," Leo added.

The timer went off in the kitchen. *Beep . . . beep . . . beep.*

Leo bounced up from his chair, went into the kitchen, and turned the soup off. He looked at the schedule on the refrigerator door, held up by a magnet of Bill Murray pointing outward with the words *You are awesome* on it.

Newport High School
Junior Varsity Football Schedule
All games are on Thursdays at 3:30 p.m.

September 24	Manchester HS
October 1	at Riverside HS
October 8	Marshall HS
October 15	at Jackson HS
October 22	at Milford HS
October 29	Fairport HS
November 5	at Clinton HS
November 12	Kingston HS

"You really should come to the game on

Thursday," Leo shouted into the living room. "We're playing at home, and who knows? You might see me score a touchdown."

"Maybe," Mom said above the music.

Chapter
FOURTEEN

"Did you hear the news?" Hank asked Leo and Sebby as they put on their equipment for Monday's practice.

Leo shook his head. "No, what?"

"Jake Healy is back."

"It's about time," Sebby said. "How long does a sprained ankle take to heal, anyway?"

"Long time, I guess," Leo said. "I heard it was a high-ankle sprain."

"Wonder if Coach K. will put him in to run back kicks," Hank added.

Leo was wondering the same thing. He could feel his chance of finally scoring a touchdown slipping away. The Newport JV team had only one more game left in its season. If Leo did not return kicks . . .

"Maybe he'll keep Leo in," Sebby suggested. "He's done all right."

"What do you mean all right?" Leo said. The words had stung. "I've had some good returns."

Hank finished tying up his cleats. "We'll find out soon enough. Let's go."

About halfway through the practice, Coach K. called the kickoff return team together.

"Look who's coming over," Leo whispered to Sebby, motioning to a player jogging to the circle. "Jake."

"Hope you're not out of a job," Sebby said.

Coach K. held his hands up for quiet. "Kingston High School is always a tough team, so the special teams may have to make some big plays."

He slapped Jake's shoulder pads. "Jake is back one hundred percent from his ankle injury, so I am going to have him handle the kickoff and punt return duties."

Some of the players clapped but Leo just nodded. He was glad he was wearing his helmet so Coach K. and the other guys couldn't see the disappointed look on his face.

Coach continued. "But now that we have two guys who can run back kicks—Jake and Leo—I thought we would put in a new kick-off return play that might catch the Kingston team by surprise. Get in tight; I want to show you the play."

The Raiders' special teams players pressed in closer to their coach, who held a tablet above the group. A diagram of the new play appeared on the screen.

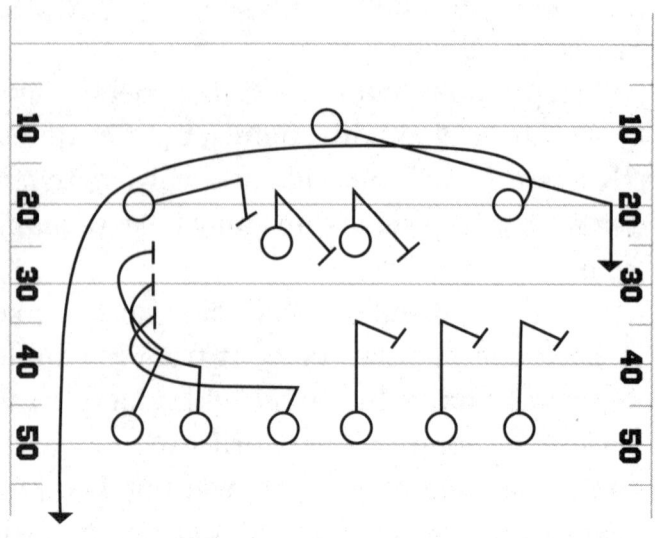

Coach began to explain the play as he

pointed to the screen. "Jake will line up at around the ten-yard line. Leo will line up on the left side with the group of blockers around the twenty-yard line."

Leo picked out the spot where he would be lining up as Coach continued to describe the play. "Everything goes like our regular kickoff-return-left play, except . . . instead of blocking, Leo will loop back to the right to take a handoff from Jake and run it down the right sideline. Any questions?"

"What do the blockers do after the handoff? Keep blocking left?" Sebby called out.

"Good question. After the handoff is made, blockers should try to pick up someone and push them toward the left side. Hopefully they will all be running that way, thinking Jake has the ball. Be careful not to block anyone in the back. That's a penalty."

Coach looked around the huddle. "Okay, let's run it."

The special teams players lined up in their usual places for the kickoff return, except that Jake was the only return man and Leo was lined up with the blockers in front of him. Coach tossed the ball downfield to start the play.

Jake caught the ball at the 10-yard line and started running left. Just as the play was diagrammed, when Jake caught the ball, Leo spun back to take a handoff. He sprinted across the field and down the right sideline.

"Good!" Coach shouted. "Let's run it again."

The Newport special teams players ran the play a half dozen more times, practicing the timing and the angle of the handoff, as well as when the blockers would switch from blocking for Jake to blocking for Leo.

The ground was hard, the light was growing dim, and the air was getting cold.

"Okay," Coach called out. "I think we have time for one more."

Jake caught the ball and headed left. Leo looped back and took the handoff at full speed. In just a few steps, he was across the field. Leo cut left, sprinting down the right sideline with Hank and

Sebby leading the way.

Tweeeeeeet! Coach blew his whistle to end the play.

"Perfect. I like the way Jake and Leo made the exchange." Leo could see Coach smiling even in the dying light. "And I love how Harris and Bates hustled over to get in front of the runner. That's it. Hit the showers."

Leo, Sebby, and Hank walked off the practice field together.

"It's too bad Jake is running back kicks instead of you," Sebby said. "But that new kickoff play is pretty cool."

"Do you think it will work?" Leo asked, thinking back to the play.

"It could," Hank said, lifting his helmet off his head. "Like Coach said, it's got to be a good kick."

"Yeah," Leo agreed. "Jake can't let the kick bounce or that will mess up the timing on the handoff. He's got to catch it in the air."

"And if he does . . ." Hank smiled looking at Leo. "You might just have a chance to score a touchdown."

Leo stopped and thrust both hands into the air as if he had already scored.

The three friends laughed and walked out of the cold and into the locker room.

Chapter
FIFTEEN

The stadium lights were already on when the teams from Newport and Kingston high schools trotted onto the field.

Leo looked around. There was a good crowd even though the temperature was dropping fast. Most of the leaves on the trees beyond the stadium fence had fallen to the ground.

Both of his parents were sitting halfway up the stands at the 50-yard line with a cluster of other parents. His mom had agreed to come to the game but had made Leo promise he "wouldn't get hurt." Leo promised, although both he and his mom knew anything could happen in a football game.

Coach Carter called the team together.

"We're going to need forty minutes of full-speed football to beat these guys!" he shouted, his breath coming out in puffs of mist as he held up four fingers. "All four quarters."

Jake ran back the opening kickoff to the 31-yard line. Leo stood on the sidelines thinking, *That was okay but not great.*

The Raiders and Kingston Hawks settled into a hard-fought game. The Hawks scored first, powered by a series of runs by their star running back, J. J. Pulasky. The Newport defense stopped the two-point try by gang-tackling Pulasky on a sweep. But Kingston led 6–0.

"Man, that guy is tough to stop," Leo said as he flopped on to the bench.

"That's why we all have to help out," Sebby said. "No way one guy can bring him down."

The Raiders came back to score near the end of the second quarter. They grabbed the lead when Jamar dove and snagged a pass for the two-point conversion.

Newport led 8–6 at the half.

In the second half, the Raiders' defense

struggled to stop Pulasky. The teams traded touchdowns and two-point conversions. Newport clung to a 16–14 lead as the game went into the final quarter.

The Hawks got the ball early in the fourth quarter and began a grinding drive that ate up yardage and time. Kingston was at the 20-yard line and threatening to score.

"Come on, we got to stop them!" Sebby shouted from in back of the Raiders' defensive line.

Sebby and three other Raider defenders met Pulasky near the line of scrimmage, stopping him for a one-yard gain. It was second down and nine yards to go.

The Hawks quarterback faked the ball to Pulasky and gained three yards on a keeper. Now it was third and six at the 16-yard line.

Leo lined up one-on-one against the Hawks' wide receiver. *I've got to be ready,* he thought. *They may try a pass.*

Sure enough, the quarterback faked to Pulasky and faded back to pass. The wide receiver went downfield five yards and faked as if he were going to the sideline, but then spun upfield. Leo did not fall for the fake and ran step-for-step with him to the end zone.

The Kingston quarterback let go a high pass for the corner of the end zone. It was a fifty-fifty ball. Leo and the wide receiver went up together, both reaching out for the football. The Hawks' wide receiver was just a couple inches taller than Leo. His fingers touched the ball first and ripped it away from Leo as they tumbled into the corner of the end zone, the wide receiver pressing the ball against his shoulder pads.

"He's out of bounds!" Sebby shouted as he stood over the two players. "He's out of bounds!"

Leo looked around, hoping the line judge would agree with the Raiders' linebacker. But after a moment's hesitation, the line judge pushed his hands over his head.

Touchdown!

The wide receiver untangled himself from Leo, popped to his feet, and slammed the ball into the end zone turf in celebration.

Leo stood by helplessly as the Hawks

danced in the end zone. *I had him covered,* he thought, *but he still got the ball.*

Coach K. was on the field, clapping and shouting at his defense. "Come on, Raiders. Need a big play. We got to stop the extra point."

Coach was right. If the Hawks made the two-point conversion, they would be up by six points and the Raiders would need a touchdown *and* a two-point conversion after the touchdown to win.

The Hawks' quarterback handed the ball to Pulasky, but the Hawks' star runner met a wall of tacklers who stopped him at the line of scrimmage. The score was 20–16; Kingston was ahead by only four points.

Leo, Sebby, and the rest of the Raiders' defense celebrated the stop. But as Leo walked off the field, he looked up at the lights of the scoreboard.

VISITOR			HOME
20	2:15	QTR 4	16

The Raiders were behind with only a little more than two minutes to play. "We need a big play," Leo whispered to himself.

Chapter
SIXTEEN

"Kickoff team! Kickoff team!" Coach K. shouted as the defense came off the field. "Over here, right now."

The members of the special teams kickoff unit huddled around their coach. Coach K. bent over as if he wanted to keep his words in the circle. "We are going to run that kickoff reverse play we practiced this week."

Leo's heart almost jumped out of his chest. He was going to get the ball!

"Does everyone remember what they are supposed to do on the play?" Coach asked, looking around at his players. The circle of helmets nodded as Coach continued, "Good. Remember, we only run the play if Jake catches the ball in the air. If the ball hits the ground, it's a straight kickoff-return-left play."

The Newport special teamers were already drifting out to line up for the kick. Jake stood in the middle of the field on the 10-yard line. Leo jogged over to his position, closer to the left sideline around the 20-yard line, and took a deep breath.

The kick was perfect, high and deep, forcing Jake to field the ball at the 5-yard line. Leo drifted back as though he were forming a line of blockers with his teammates. Just as they had practiced, the other blockers moved left as Jake started running hard to that side of the field.

Instead of blocking, Leo looped back and took the handoff from Jake at the 15-yard line. He dodged a Kingston tackler as he raced across the field. Then he turned on the burners and sprinted down the sidelines as his blockers, including Sebby and Hank, gave him room to run.

Leo sidestepped another Hawks tackler at midfield and lost his balance for a moment, but he regained his stride.

His heart leaped. There was nothing but open field in front of him and the end zone!

He was at the forty . . . the thirty . . .

Then out of nowhere, one last Hawks defender who had been racing after Leo leaped in one final desperate attempt to bring him down. His hand yanked at the arm where Leo cradled the football.

The tip of the ball slipped from Leo's palm and bumped against his pads as Leo lost his balance and started to tumble. The ball popped loose before Leo hit the ground.

Fumble!

Leo was on the ground, tangled up with the Hawks' tackler. He twisted to see the football turning end over end along the sideline grass.

On the third bounce, the ball popped higher in the air just as Hank, who had been following the play, rushed after the ball and snapped it out of the air. Leo watched from the grass as the big lineman rumbled down the sideline with the ball safely tucked in his beefy arms. Sebby followed, checking the field for any Kingston tacklers.

There were none left, and Hank ran the final yards untouched into the end zone. He held his arms and the football above his head in triumph.

Touchdown! The Raiders led 22–20.

Leo scrambled to his feet to join his teammates shouting in the end zone.

"What a play!"

"Did you see the big guy run?"

"Great hustle!"

Coach Carter stepped out on the field and tried to bring his team back to earth. "Come on, we still have about two minutes to go. We need one last stop."

The Raiders' trick play touchdown seemed to have drained the energy from the Kingston team. After two incompletions, a screen pass gained only one yard. It was fourth down with nine yards to go for a first down.

The Hawks' quarterback faded back to pass, but the Raiders' defensive linemen crashed in for a final sack. It was the Raiders' ball with time running out. The Newport quarterback knelt down and let the final seconds melt away.

The Raiders had won!

After the final whistle, the teams milled around the field shaking hands. The parents and other fans came down on the field because it was the last game of the season.

Leo walked over to his mom and dad after he spotted them in the crowd.

"We won!" he called out, almost forgetting his last-minute fumble. He pushed his helmet toward the darkened skies.

"I'm just glad you kept your promise and didn't get hurt," his mother said as she put her arms around his shoulder pads.

"I told you," his father shouted as he came closer, his smile brightened by the stadium lights. "There are a lot of ways to score in a football game."

Leo laughed. "I know, but I never thought in a million years *Hank* would be the one scoring."

Chapter
SEVENTEEN

"Man, it's packed," Leo said as he looked around the Newport High School football field.

"The Turkey Day Classic game against Webster is always crowded," Sebby said. "It's a Thanksgiving tradition."

"I told you we should have gotten here earlier," Ginny said.

"Okay, okay, you told us," Leo admitted, scanning the stands.

Hank pointed to a corner of the stadium. "I think there are some seats up there."

The four friends squeezed into a small space in the last row of the stadium and settled in to watch the game.

Leo rubbed his hands together. "Well, at

least we won't get cold. We're packed in here plenty tight."

Down on the field, the Newport and Webster varsity teams were locked in their hard-fought traditional game.

Newport jumped out to a quick 7–0 lead on a long touchdown pass followed by a point-after-touchdown kick. But the Webster Patriots came back with a drive that ended with a fifteen-yard sweep around the right end. The score was tied, 7–7.

As the Raiders' varsity lined up to receive the kickoff, Sebby wondered out loud, "Maybe they'll try the reverse play. After all, it worked for us."

"Yeah," Leo said. "But I fumbled. Remember?"

"You didn't fumble," Hank insisted.

"What are you talking about?" Leo said, looking at the lineman in surprise. "I lost the ball, didn't I?"

Hank grinned as he put his arm around Leo. "That, my friend, was not a fumble. It was an assist."

They all laughed and then turned their

attention back to the game. The score was knotted 14–14 at halftime. Leo looked at Ginny as the Newport band played "We Are the Champions" on the field.

"So, how many touchdowns did you end up with this season?"

Ginny shook her head. "I don't know."

Leo's head snapped back. "You don't know?"

"I know I had more than Hank," she laughed as she elbowed the big lineman.

"No really," Leo insisted. "How many touchdowns? I saw you score four against Marshall. I'm sure you had more than that."

Ginny looked out at the field. The teams were coming back for the second half.

"We played eight games. I guess I averaged about two touchdowns a game. So fifteen or sixteen touchdowns for the year."

Leo shook his head. "You scored so many touchdowns, you can't even remember how many you scored."

"I know our team's record was six and two."

"We were seven and one," Sebby interrupted. "We beat you there."

The Newport defense stopped Webster when the Raiders' cornerback broke up a third-down pass and forced the Patriots to punt.

Ginny looked back at Leo. "So, how many passes did you break up this year?"

"I don't . . ." Leo started to answer, but Ginny cut him short.

"How many times did the quarterback not even throw to your man because you had him covered?"

"I don't know, but . . ."

"How many tackles did you have?"

Sebby laughed and joined in. "Not as many as me, I can tell you that."

"How many did you have?" Leo asked.

"One hundred and thirteen . . . and a half." Sebby could see the shock on Leo's face. "I'm kidding," he said. "I didn't count them."

"Yeah," Hank chuckled. "That's because he can't count that high."

"I'll bet Coach Carter is counting tackles," Ginny said. "And the passes you break up and all kinds of stats." She looked down at the field and continued, "Listen, I'm just saying all that stuff—breaking up passes, making tackles . . ."

"Don't forget blocking," Hank added.

"Blocking . . . all that stuff is just as important as scoring touchdowns."

"Yeah, but . . ." Leo started.

"But nothing. Different kids . . . different talents . . . different positions," Ginny said firmly. "You need everybody on a football team. Including a flag football team."

Leo could almost hear his mother's voice. *Sometimes you don't get to choose your talents.*

On the field, the Newport quarterback faded back and let fly a long pass to a Newport receiver who had a step on the defender. For a moment the pass looked overthrown, but the receiver seemed to speed up to get under the football. He grabbed the ball and sprinted untouched down the sideline. The crowd jumped to its feet as the wide receiver crossed the goal line for a touchdown.

"You're going to have to get a lot better at catching passes if you want that guy's job," Hank shouted to Leo over the cheering crowd.

Leo stared down at the players celebrating in the end zone. The Raiders' wide receiver held the ball in triumph above the crowd. Leo thought back on the past season. The tryouts for wide receiver. Coach breaking up the team into offense, defense, and special teams. The drills. Learning to play cornerback . . . and kick returner. The ups, the downs, and the almost-touchdown he fumbled away.

"Yeah, you're probably right," Leo said with a knowing smile. "But I bet you anything I can cover that guy."

THE REAL STORY

In football, most touchdowns are scored in two ways. First, a team can score on the simplest offensive play in the game. That's when a player gives the ball to another player and lets him run it into the end zone. Second, a player (usually the quarterback) throws the ball to a receiver who takes it in for the score.

That's why Leo wanted to be a wide receiver. Wide receivers catch passes and score touchdowns.

But there are other ways to score touchdowns.

Special teams players can catch punts or kickoffs and zigzag through the other team all the way to the end zone. Or a defensive player can intercept a pass and return it for a score. That's called a "pick-six." And, as Hank showed, sometimes a player can recover a fumble and take it all the way.

Finally, although it doesn't happen very often, a player can take a blocked kick or a missed field goal and return it for a touchdown.

Over the years there have been some players who have been very good at scoring "non-offensive" touchdowns (N-OTD). Let's take another look at that list of players Leo and his father found on Pro-Football-Reference.com.

PLAYER	N-OTD	YEARS
Devin Hester	20	2006-2016
Deion Sanders	19	1989-2005
Ron Woodson	17	1987-2003
Ronde Barber	14	1997-2012
Brian Mitchell	13	1990-2003

An elusive runner with breakaway speed, Devin Hester scored six touchdowns on kick returns when he was at the University of Miami. Hester took the National Football League (NFL) by storm when he came out of college in 2006. He scored an unbelievable eleven touchdowns on punt and kickoff returns in his first two NFL seasons.

Hester's production slowed down some, but he finished his career with an NFL-record fourteen punt returns for touchdowns as well as five scoring kickoff returns. And yes, Hester even returned a missed field goal all the way back for a score.

For all these touchdowns and his spectacular runbacks on special teams, Hester was inducted into the Pro Football Hall of Fame in 2024.

The next three names on the list were terrific defensive backs who also found ways into the end zone.

"Neon Deion" Sanders was a flashy player who, as Leo said, found almost every way to score. Here's the list of Sanders' career non-offensive scoring plays:

Pick-six interceptions	9
Punt returns for TDs	6
Kickoff returns for TDs	3
Fumble recoveries for TDs	1

Sanders also caught three passes for touchdowns. The only way Sanders did not score, according to pro-football-reference.com, was on a running play.

Woodson intercepted seventy-one passes during his sixteen-year career, including a record twelve that he took back for scores. Early in his career, while playing for the Pittsburgh Steelers, the athletic Woodson also returned punts and kickoffs and brought back a total of four for touchdowns.

Barber was not quite the scorer Woodson was, but the defensive stalwart for the Tampa Bay Buccaneers returned eight interceptions, four fumbles, and one punt for touchdowns during his sixteen-year career. He is also the twin brother of Tiki Barber, a star running back for the New York Giants from 1997 to 2006.

The first four players on the list—Hester, Sanders, Woodson, and Barber—have been selected for the Pro Football Hall of Fame. The last name on the list—Brian Mitchell—is not in the Hall of Fame, but maybe he should be.

Mitchell was a do-everything running back for

the Washington Redskins (now Commanders). He was mostly a super substitute and a special teams player. Mitchell only started sixteen games during his fourteen-year career. But he found ways to help his team.

Mitchell ran with the football, caught passes, and returned punts and kickoffs. In fact, when you add up all the yards Mitchell gained for his teams (he also played for the Philadelphia Eagles and New York Giants late in his career), he gained more all-purpose yards (23,330) than any player in NFL history other than legendary wide receiver Jerry Rice (23,546).

One last name that should be mentioned in any discussion of players who found different ways to score is Bill Dudley. An All-American from the University of Virginia, Dudley was someone who could do just about everything on a football field. During his nine-year career in the NFL (1942–1953), Dudley is the only player who scored in seven (!) different ways.

A running back, Dudley scored on runs (eighteen career TDs) and pass receptions (eighteen). He also returned three punts and one kickoff for scores.

Early in his career, Dudley also played defensive back at a time when many players played both offense and defense. As a defender, Dudley intercepted twenty-seven passes and returned two for touchdowns. He also recovered seventeen fumbles and returned one for a score.

If all this was not enough, the amazing Dudley appears to have taken a lateral from a teammate who had blocked a kick and ran the ball back for a touchdown. He also threw passes, punted, and kicked field goals and extra points.

Dudley might have scored even more touchdowns, but he served in the Army Air Corps in the Pacific during the later years of World War II.

As Leo's father said, "There are a lot of ways to score in football." Some players have found them all.

ACKNOWLEDGMENTS

The information about the careers and scoring exploits of NFL players Devin Hester, Deion Sanders, Rod Woodson, Rondee Barber, Brian Mitchell, and Bill Dudley come from the indispensable website Pro-Football-Reference.com.

The various drills for defensive backs described in the book were found on several training videos posted on YouTube. Thank you to all the football coaches who share their knowledge about the game online.

The kickoff return diagram was drawn by my friend and former colleague at the Department of Labor, Steve Willertz. Steve is currently an assistant coach for the freshman football team at Archbishop Spalding High School in Severn, Maryland.

ABOUT THE AUTHOR

Fred Bowen was a Little Leaguer who loved to read. Now he is the author of many action-packed books of sports fiction. He wrote a weekly sports column for kids for *The Washington Post* from 2000–2023.

Fred played lots of sports growing up, including soccer at Marblehead High School. For thirteen years, he coached kids' baseball, soccer, and basketball teams. Some of his stories spring directly from his coaching experience and his sports-happy childhood in Marblehead, Massachusetts.

Fred holds a degree in history from the University of Pennsylvania and a law degree from George Washington University. He was a lawyer for many years before retiring to become a full-time children's author. Bowen has been a guest author at schools and conferences across the country, as well as the National Book Festival in Washington, DC, and the Baseball Hall of Fame.

Fred lives in Silver Spring, Maryland, with his wife, Peggy Jackson. Their son is head baseball coach at the University of Maryland, Baltimore County, and their daughter is a school librarian in Washington, DC.

For more information, check out the author's website at FredBowen.com.

ABOUT THE COVER ILLUSTRATOR

Marcelo Baez, an illustrator and comics artist, is creating new cover illustrations for all the titles in the Fred Bowen Sports Story series. Marcelo has worked for Marvel, *ESPN the Magazine*, and Scholastic, just to name a few. He was born in Chile and lives in Australia.

HEY, SPORTS FANS!

Don't miss these action-packed books in the Fred Bowen Sports Story series!

Ebook editions also available

BASEBALL

DUGOUT RIVALS
PB: 978-1-56145-515-7
Last year Jake was one of his team's best players. But this season it looks like a new kid is going to take Jake's place as team leader. Can Jake settle for second best?

EXTRA INNINGS
PB: 978-1-68263-784-5
HC: 978-1-68263-411-0
Mike loves pitching, but his father wants Mike to spend the summer working. Can Mike and his father reach a compromise so that Mike can help his team win the end-of-summer tournament?

THE GOLDEN GLOVE
PB: 978-1-56145-505-8
Without his lucky glove, Jamie doesn't believe in his ability to lead his baseball team to victory. How will he learn that faith in oneself is the most important equipment for any game?

THE KID COACH
PB: 978-1-56145-506-5
Scott and his teammates can't find an adult to coach their team, so they must find a leader among themselves.

LUCKY ENOUGH
PB: 978-1-56145-958-2
When Trey's good-luck charm helps him make the Ravens travel team, it reinforces his superstitious behavior. For a while his hitting and fielding get better and better. But one day his lucky charm goes missing and his performance on the team starts to slip. Is his future with the Ravens doomed?

PLAYOFF DREAMS
PB: 978-1-56145-507-2
Brendan is one of the best players in the league, but no matter how hard he tries, he can't make his team win.

T.J.'S SECRET PITCH
PB: 978-1-56145-504-1
T.J.'s pitches just don't pack the power they need to strike out the batters, but the story of 1940s baseball hero Rip Sewell and his legendary eephus pitch may help him find a solution.

THROWING HEAT
PB: 978-1-56145-540-9
HC: 978-1-56145-573-7
Jack throws the fastest pitches around, but lately his blazing fastballs haven't been enough. He's got to learn new pitches to stay ahead of the batters. But can he resist bringing the heat?

WINNERS TAKE ALL
PB: 978-1-56145-512-6
Kyle makes a poor decision to cheat in a big game. Someone discovers the truth and threatens to reveal it. What can Kyle do now?

BASKETBALL

THE FINAL CUT
PB: 978-1-56145-510-2
Four friends realize that they may not all make the team and that the tryouts are a test—not only of their athletic skills, but also of their friendship.

FULL COURT FEVER
PB: 978-1-56145-508-9
The Falcons have the skill but not the height to win their games. Will the full-court zone press be the solution to their problem?

HARDCOURT COMEBACK
PB: 978-1-56145-516-4
Brett blew a key play in an important game. Now he feels like a loser for letting his teammates down—and he keeps making mistakes. How can Brett become a "winner" again?

OFF THE BENCH
PB: 978-1-68263-524-7
HC: 978-1-68263-410-3
Kris dreams of being part of his basketball team's starting lineup, but the new coach has other plans, using Kris as his valuable "sixth man." But how can Kris be the high scorer he dreams of if he's not a starter?

OFF THE RIM
PB: 978-1-56145-509-6
Hoping to be more than a benchwarmer, Chris learns that defense is just as important as offense.

ON THE LINE
PB: 978-1-56145-511-9
Marcus is the highest scorer and the best rebounder, but he's not so great at free throws—until the school custodian helps him overcome his fear of failure.

OUTSIDE SHOT
PB: 978-1-56145-956-8
Richie has always known he was a shooter. He practices every day at his driveway hoop, perfecting his technique. Now that he is facing basketball tryouts under a tough new coach, will his amazing shooting talent be enough to keep him on the team?

REAL HOOPS
PB: 978-1-56145-566-9
Hud can run, pass, and shoot at top speed. But he's not much of a team player. Can Ben convince Hud to leave his dazzling—but one-man—style back on the asphalt?

FOOTBALL

DOUBLE REVERSE
PB: 978-1-56145-807-3
The season starts off badly, and things get even worse when the Panthers quarterback is injured. Jesse knows the playbook by heart, but he feels he is too small for the role. Can he play against type and help the Panthers become a winning team?

QUARTERBACK SEASON
PB: 978-1-56145-594-2
Matt expects to be the starting quarterback. But after a few practices watching Devro, a talented seventh grader, he's starting to get nervous. To make matters worse, his English teacher is on his case about a new class assignment: a journal.

SPEED DEMON
PB: 978-1-68263-077-8
Eager to find his place at his elite new school, ninth-grader Tim Beeman is torn between running track and trying out for football. Where will he feel most comfortable and be able to put his fast running skills to best use?

TOUCHDOWN TROUBLE
PB: 978-1-56145-497-6
Thanks to a major play by Sam, the Cowboys beat their archrivals to remain undefeated. But the celebration ends when Sam and his teammates make an unexpected discovery. Is their perfect season in jeopardy?

SOCCER

GO FOR THE GOAL!
PB: 978-1-56145-632-1
Josh and his talented travel league soccer teammates are having trouble coming together as a successful team—until he convinces them to try team-building exercises.

SOCCER TEAM UPSET
PB: 978-1-56145-495-2
Tyler is angry when his team's star player leaves to join an elite travel team. Just as Tyler expected, the Cougars' season goes straight downhill. Can he make a difference before it's too late?

SOCCER TROPHY MYSTERY
PB: 978-1-68263-079-2
HC: 978-1-68263-078-5
Soccer-playing twins Aiden and Ava are devoted to the game, and they are both playing hard to lead their teams to a championship season. Still, they find the time to try to unravel the long-standing mystery of their town's missing soccer trophy